To Eliana.

MIX
Paper from responsible sources
FSC® C101807

Whatever Happened to My Sister © Flying Eye Books 2015.

This is a first edition published in 2015 by Flying Eye Books,
an imprint of Nobrow Ltd. 62 Great Eastern Street, London, EC2A 3QR.

Published in the US by Nobrow (US) Inc.
Printed in Belgium on FSC assured paper.

ISBN: 978-1-909263-52-9

Order from www.flyingeyebooks.com

Simona Ciraolo

Whatever happened to my sister?

Flying Eye Books
London – New York

I'd had my suspicions for a while

that someone had
replaced my sister with a girl
who looked a lot like her.

It had to be!

My sister was never so tall.

Did it happen overnight?

I am rather observant, yet the moment
of the switch must have passed me by.

I suppose there
were the signs.

She'd been incredibly
boring on several occasions

but I guess I didn't
give it much thought...

...at least until I noticed her sense of fashion had gone.
This new sister showed no interest in pretty things.

It all became very odd.
She began acting all secretive
(even when it wasn't close to my birthday).

And she developed the annoying habit
of always keeping her bedroom door shut.

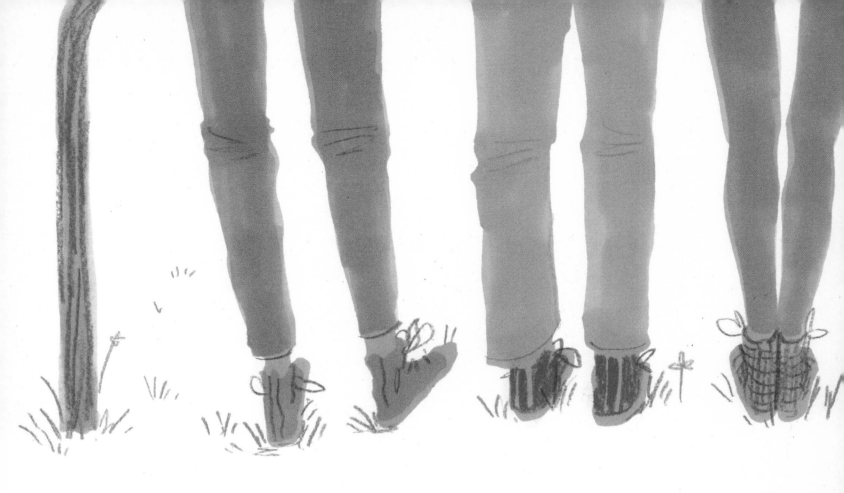

That's when I started to worry. I made up my
mind to see if her friends had some answers...

...but something wasn't right with them either.

And it wasn't just that a lot of them were boys.

I was sure my mum knew something
because I saw them scheming in her bedroom.

My dad must have suspected something, too.
But when I asked if he had noticed anything
strange, he just looked at the ceiling, muttering.

One day, as I was putting together
all my clues, I began to think about when
my sister used to tell me everything.

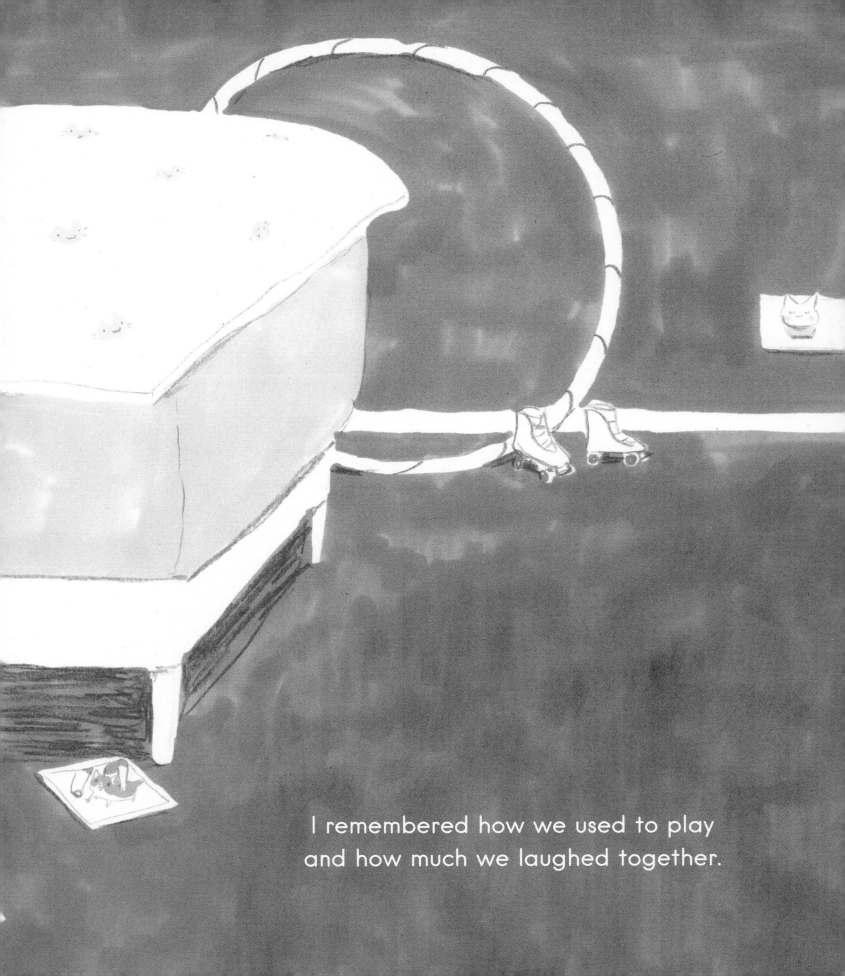

I remembered how we used to play
and how much we laughed together.

And it made me realise

how much I missed her.

That's when my sister found me,

and told me to come with her.

She put on some music
and we listened to it together.

It was after a while that she
stopped to look at me and asked,
"When did YOU become so tall?"